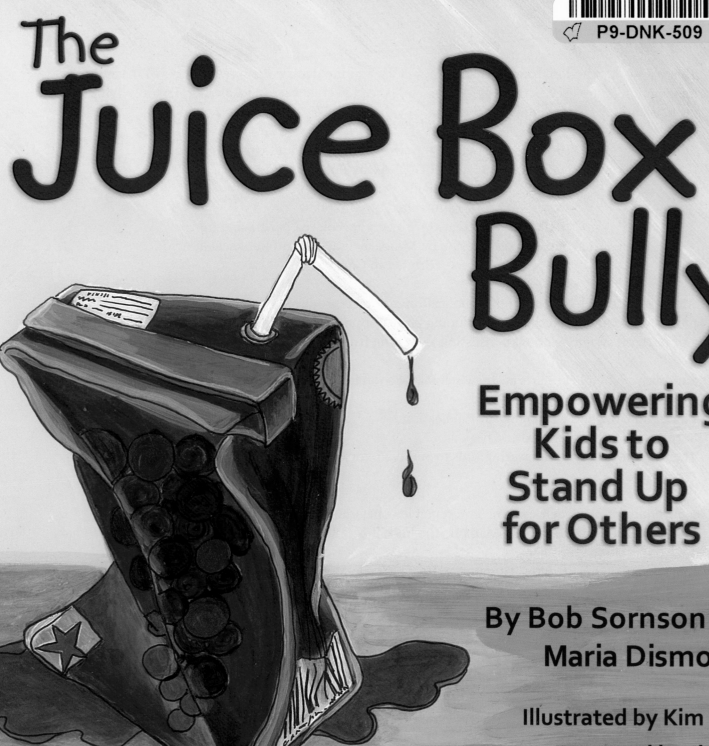

The Juice Box Bully

Empowering Kids to Stand Up for Others

By Bob Sornson and
Maria Dismondy

Illustrated by Kim Shaw

Foreword by Jim Fay
Co-Founder of the Love and Logic Institute

The Juice Box Bully: Empowering Kids to Stand Up for Others
Copyright © 2011 by Bob Sornson
Eighth Printing 2017
Illustrated by Kim Shaw
Illustrations created with acrylic, colored pencil, and ink
Layout and cover design by Kimberly Franzen and Raphael Giuffrida
Printed in Canada

Summary: When Pete starts at a new school, he soon finds out that being a bystander to bad behavior is not tolerated.

Library of Congress Cataloging-in-Publication Data
Sornson, Bob and Dismondy, Maria
The Juice Box Bully: Empowering Kids to Stand Up for Others/Bob Sornson and Maria Dismondy–
First Edition
ISBN-13: 978-1-933916-72-9
1. Juvenile fiction. 2. Self-esteem. 3. Acceptable behavior. 4. No bystanders. 5. Bullying.
I. Sornson, Bob and Dismondy, Maria II. The Juice Box Bully: Empowering Kids to Stand Up for Others

Library of Congress Control Number: 2010932349

EARLY LEARNING
FOUNDATION
5985 Hartford Way
Brighton, MI 48116
earlylearningfoundation.com
(810) 775-3646

It is a special honor to write the foreword to *The Juice Box Bully: Empowering Kids to Stand Up for Others*, written by Bob Sornson and Maria Dismondy. Classroom culture plays a significant part in reducing bullying. Teachers can help children develop the skills and values that will enable them to learn to respectfully set limits and eliminate bullying.

I hope that teachers and parents share this book with their kids to provide a positive example of these skills and values in action. Children can help bullies understand that their bullying behaviors will not endear them to the group. Children can set a clear standard for appropriate behavior and help us all learn that fear and intimidation are not the best ways to gain status.

Every child who learns through this book will make the world better, for themselves as well as for others. Imagine the difference this can make.

Respectfully,
Jim Fay, Co-Founder of the Love and Logic Institute,
Co-Author of *Parenting with Love and Logic*

To my children, Rebecca, Matt, Alicia, and Molly. You inspire me to learn how to set limits with respect and love. I am blessed to have you in my life. B.S.

To my parents, with gratitude, and to my Little Ruby, with endless love. M.D.

We would like to acknowledge teachers and parents everywhere who are working hard to teach children to stand up and create a respectful culture in their communities.

As Pete stood in front of his new class, Mr. Peltzer announced, "Let's welcome Pete to our team. Pete, you will be sitting behind Ralph."

Settling into his seat, Pete pulled his hat down over his head so that only his eyes could be seen. Turning around, Ralph warned him, "They don't allow hats in class here."
"You're not my mother," snarled Pete.

After giving an assignment, Mr. Peltzer walked around the class and quietly asked Pete to remove his hat. Once he walked away, Pete poked Ralph. "Thanks a lot," he growled.

Later that day at recess, Pete didn't ask to join the soccer game. Instead, he watched.

"Hi, Pete," Ralph said. "Do you want to get into the game?"
"Not with those nerds," Pete replied. "I don't like those kids."
"What do you want to do?" asked Ralph.

Pete smiled spitefully. "Let's steal the ball. We're bigger than them. We can have our own game."

"I don't think so," answered Ralph. "That's not how we do things around here."

"Then I'll do it myself," taunted Pete, "if you're so afraid."

Pete ran over to the field and yelled, "Pass it to me!" When David passed the soccer ball, Pete grabbed it and ran off the field.

"What's going on?" shouted David.

Pete didn't answer. He ran faster and faster, then turned and waved the ball in the air.

At first, the kids just stood there. Then they huddled together before walking over to Pete. Ruby and Lucy led the way.

"I know you're new around here, but what are you doing?" asked Ruby.

"I'm playing with the soccer ball," Pete snapped. "Think you're going to take it away from me?"

Ruby didn't argue, nor did she threaten Pete. Instead, she softly but firmly explained, "It's your first day here, so there is no way you could know this. In Mr. Peltzer's class, we made a promise."

"We promised to take care of ourselves, each other, and our classroom, and to solve problems peacefully. We promised that in this class, no one would stand by and accept bad behavior.

When someone acts hurtfully, we all speak up. We want you to be a member of the class and to make the same promise."

"Dumb rules. Dumb promises."
Throwing the ball to the ground, Pete walked away.

The next day, Pete ate alone. When he finished lunch, the kids raced out of the lunchroom while Pete trailed behind. Ruby ran up to Pete and asked, "Do you want to play soccer today?"
"I don't play with nerds."
"Okey dokey," Ruby replied.

"Hey, Ruby," Pete called after her.
Ruby stopped and turned. "Nice shirt," Pete complimented,
then he squirted his juice box right at her.

"You are so mean!" she shrieked at him. "I'll tell everyone how mean you are. You won't have any friends here!"

By now Ralph, David, and some others had come up to them. "Ruby, I won't let you do that," Ralph said clearly. "Remember our promise?"

"I don't want to remember the promise. Look what he did! We'll ignore him forever, until he leaves this school and goes back to his old school," Ruby demanded.

Ralph walked between Ruby and Pete. "We're not going to do this, Ruby. I know you're angry. You can tell Mr. Peltzer if you want, but we're not going to let you treat Pete like this. And we won't put up with his bad behavior either."

Ruby stomped away, leaving Pete and Ralph behind.
"No one's ever done that before," Pete said. "Why did you stand up for me?"
"I've been in your shoes, and I learned being a bully doesn't work."

"And, I'm not a bystander," Ralph said. "I don't stand by and let mean things happen. Besides, Ruby is my friend, and you shouldn't have ruined her shirt."

"Won't the other kids be mad at you for sticking up for me?" Pete asked.

"No way. They all made the same promise. We talked about it for a long time with Mr. Peltzer and every kid here tries to keep that promise."

"At my old school, I got picked on all the time," Pete said.
"Everybody just let it happen. So I started to tease kids
before they could be mean to me."

Ralph replied, "We decided that when somebody tries to be a bully, no one will stand by and let it happen. We speak up, or we ask for help from an adult. But we won't be bystanders to bad behavior."

The bell rang, and it was time to go back to class.
"They hate me. They'll never let me play with them," Pete said.
Before Ralph could answer, David, Lucy, and Ruby came toward them.

"I'm sorry about what I said," Ruby apologized. "I can't believe I forgot the reason why we made the promise. If we can remember to stand up for each other, school is a lot more fun!"

"Wow, the kids here are way different than at my other school," Pete said. "Maybe I'll give this promise thing a try."

"Great! Let's go talk to Mr. Peltzer," said Ruby.

"Hey, Ruby, sorry about your shirt," Pete added.
Ruby smiled. "No worries, I kind of like the new look!"
Everyone laughed as Pete and Ruby led the way into class.

Bystanders are children who see bullying behavior happen but do nothing about it. Bystanders make up the largest population in schools. Experts say that bystanders have the power to reduce bullying in schools by speaking up.

As adults, we can empower children to take action when they are witnessing a bullying situation. One way is to adopt and practice "The Promise," whereby children and adults are no longer bystanders. Adults need to encourage children to speak up about troubling situations and reassure them that there are adults who can help.

We encourage you to make the same promise that the children portrayed in this book did.

The Promise

I WILL speak up instead of acting as a bystander.

I CHOOSE to participate in activities that don't involve teasing.

I FORGIVE others if they make poor choices.

I MODEL good behavior.

I ACCEPT others for their differences.

I INCLUDE others in group situations.

I WILL talk to an adult when there is a problem I cannot manage on my own.

I AM powerful in making a difference in my school.

By making "The Promise" to stand up against bad behavior, we can put an end to bullying.

Stand Up!

Bob Sornson, PhD, was a classroom teacher and school administrator for over thirty years and is the founder of the Early Learning Foundation, an organization dedicated to helping schools and parents give every child an opportunity to achieve early learning success. His implementation of programs and strategies for early learning success, the *Early Learning Success Initiative*, serves as a model for districts around the country. He is committed to the belief that practically every child can have a successful early learning experience. Bob is the author of numerous articles, books, and audio recordings. His most recent book is *Creating Classrooms Where Teachers Love to Teach and Students Love to Learn* (Love and Logic Press). To contact Bob or learn more about his books, please visit www.earlylearningfoundation.com.

Melissa Mooradian Photography

Maria Dismondy is dedicated to inspiring and empowering those around her through her roles as author, teacher, community leader, and friend. She makes promises she can keep and enjoys working in her local community and beyond. Maria has a passion for life that radiates in everything she does. Maria earned her master's degree in education in 2002 and served as an elementary school teacher in the public schools for nearly ten years before transitioning into her current role as a reading interventionist. Outside of work, Maria enjoys working on projects that are centered around creativity. Maria tours the state presenting to schools on the timely topic of bullying. Her first book, *Spaghetti in a Hot Dog Bun* (Ferne Press), teaches children to have the courage to be themselves. Maria lives in southeast Michigan with her husband, Dave, and their little girl, Ruby. For more information about Maria, please visit www.mariadismondy.com.

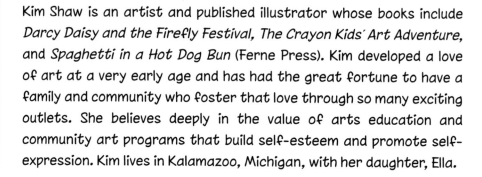

Kim Shaw is an artist and published illustrator whose books include *Darcy Daisy and the Firefly Festival*, *The Crayon Kids' Art Adventure*, and *Spaghetti in a Hot Dog Bun* (Ferne Press). Kim developed a love of art at a very early age and has had the great fortune to have a family and community who foster that love through so many exciting outlets. She believes deeply in the value of arts education and community art programs that build self-esteem and promote self-expression. Kim lives in Kalamazoo, Michigan, with her daughter, Ella.